To the memory of Francis Batten,
who spread freedom and joy wherever he went – E.M.

For Pete and Bee – P.H.

About the story

Nail Soup is retold from *Favourite Folktales from around the World,*
edited by Jane Yolen, who draws on *Scandinavian Folk and Fairy Tales*, edited by Claire Booss.
Gabriel Djurklou's *Fairy Tales from the Swedish*, translated by H.L. Bræstad,
is an even earlier source. The story sometimes features a stone or an axe,
and may involve soldiers returning from war who persuade
reluctant villagers to feed them.

Nail Soup copyright © Frances Lincoln Limited 2007
Text copyright © Eric Maddern 2007
Illustrations copyright © Paul Hess 2007

First published in Great Britain and the USA in 2007 by Frances Lincoln Children's Books,
4 Torriano Mews, Torriano Avenue, London NW5 2RZ
www.franceslincoln.com

Distributed in the USA by Publishers Group West

British Library Cataloguing in Publication Data available on request

978-1-84507-479-1

Illustrated with watercolours

Set in Oneleigh

Printed in China

1 3 5 7 9 8 6 4 2

Nail Soup

Eric Maddern

Illustrated by Paul Hess

F
FRANCES LINCOLN
CHILDREN'S BOOKS

nce long ago there was a Traveller.
Late one afternoon he was tramping along
a forest path when snowflakes began fluttering
down though the bare branches of the trees.

"Where am I going to sleep tonight?"
he wondered. "Will I have to gather my cloak around
me and nestle in the roots of the trees, or will I find
a bed?"

He rounded a bend in the path and ahead
of him was a little cottage. In the gathering dusk
he saw a candle shining in the window and thought,
"Perhaps I'll get a bed for myself here."

But at that moment out of the cottage door stepped a burly woman. Scowling at him, she planted her fists on her hips and demanded, "Who are you? Where are you going? What are you doing here?"

"Ah well," said the man, "I'm just a Traveller. I've been all round the world, I've been everywhere – except here – and now I'm on my way home."

"I see," said the woman. "But what would you be wanting here?"

"Well, I was just wondering, would there be any chance of a bed for the night?"

"Huh!" retorted the woman. "I thought as much. Well, my husband is away and this place is not an inn, so you can be on your way!"

But he wasn't the sort of fellow to give up easily, and he begged and whined and pleaded like a hungry dog. Finally she gave in.

"Well, all right," she grumbled. "You can sleep on the floor by the fire, but don't you dare ask me for anything more than that!"

"Oh no," said the Traveller:

"Better on the floor without sleep
Than suffer cold in the forest deep."

He was a merry fellow and quick with a rhyme.

The Traveller warmed himself by the fire and looked
around. She wasn't rich, but she wasn't too poor,
so after a while he said: "Any chance of a bite to eat?"

"Look!" she said. "I've got nothing in the house.
I haven't had a morsel all day long."

"In that case," said the Traveller, "I'll have
to share what I've got with you."

"What! How can anyone like you have anything
to share with me?"

"He who far away does roam
Sees many things not known at home,
And he who many things has seen
Has wits about and senses keen.
Better dead than lose your head.

Lend me a pot, granny!"

She was startled by this, and handed him an old,
black pot. He filled it with water, hung it over the fire
and stoked the coals.

As the bubbles began to rise in the pot, he reached
into his waistcoat pocket and pulled out an old,
rusty four-inch nail. He turned it round a few times,
muttering into his beard, and then dropped it,
plop! into the boiling water.

"What are you doing there?" asked the woman.

"I'm going to make… Nail Soup."

"Nail Soup!" she said. "Well, that would be
a useful thing to know how to make." And she
squatted on her haunches, eyes as wide as pumpkins,
watching him stir the nail in the pot.

After a while the Traveller said, "You know, the trouble is, I've been using this nail every day this week and the likelihood is it'll be rather thin. What would make it really good – good enough for anyone passing by – is a handful of sifted oatmeal.

But... what one has to do without,
It's no use thinking more about!"

"Well," she said, "I suppose I might have a scrap of flour somewhere." So she fetched a little sack of flour and handed it to him. He took it and shook it into the pot by the handful. And it was good flour, it was fine flour.

And as he stirred and stirred, the soup started to thicken.

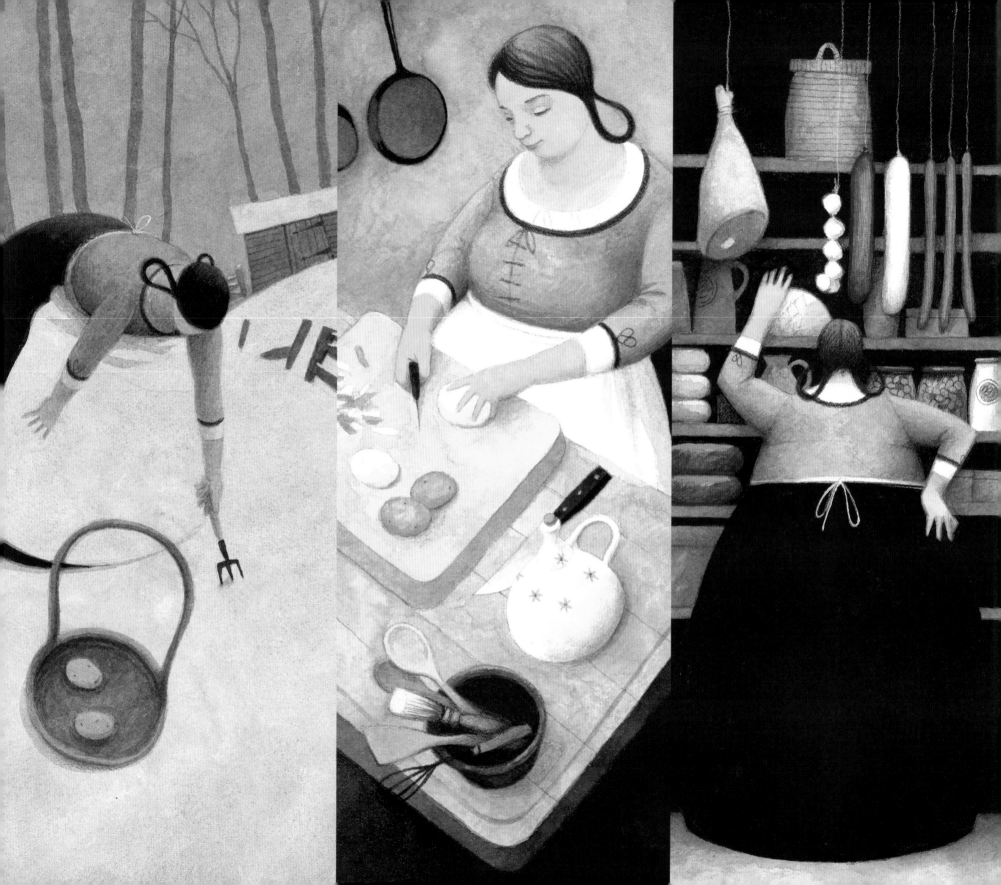

"You know," said the Traveller, "this soup would be good enough for the Lord and Lady of the manor… if only we had some potatoes and a hunk of salt beef…

But… what one has to do without,
It's no use thinking more about!"

Now she was thinking, "Well I suppose I've got some potatoes in the garden." So she went out, dug them up, washed them, peeled them, chopped them and into the pot they went. Then she went rummaging about in her pantry and found a hunk of salt beef. She chopped that up too, and into the pot it went.

And as he stirred and stirred, she thought, "Isn't he amazing! He's making soup out of a nail!"

By now, a wonderful smell was drifting around
the kitchen.

"Let me tell you something," said the Traveller.
"I used to work for the King's cook, and I know exactly
how the King and the Queen like their soup. And they
have it just like this… well, except they'd also have some
milk and barley, salt and pepper and a few herbs…

But… what one has to do without,
It's no use thinking more about!"

She was thinking, "Like the King and Queen, eh?"
So she went out, milked the goat, found some barley
in the larder, gathered a few herbs, fetched the salt
and pepper, and into the pot they went.

And as he stirred and stirred, the smell of the soup
curled under her nose and made her mouth water.

"Well, it's nearly ready," said the Traveller.
"The thing is, when the King and the Queen
have their soup, they use a fresh linen tablecloth,
their best spoons and bowls, and flowers.
They'll have a loaf of crusty bread and some good,
strong cheese and a bottle of dark red wine!

But... what one has to do without,
It's no use thinking more about!"

She was very excited now. "He could be the King,
and I'd be the Queen," she thought.

So she laid the table with her finest tablecloth,
her best spoons and bowls and some lovely flowers.
She made the rest of the flour into a loaf and baked
it in the oven. In the pantry she found some good
strong cheese and from the cellar she brought up
a bottle of dark red wine.

The Traveller reached with a spoon into the soup
and pulled out his nail. He dried it off, winked at it
and put it back in his waistcoat pocket.

Then he said, "Dinner is served!"

She put the bread and cheese on to the table.
He ladled the soup into the bowls. Then they sat down
together, said grace, and ate. And do you know,
it was the tastiest, most delicious meal she'd ever had.
Though it was simple, it had a special, magical
ingredient that made it so good...

After they'd finished the soup, the bread and
the cheese, they drank the dark red wine. It seemed
to loosen their tongues and he told her stories
of his travels around the world. By the end of
the evening, she was even remembering a few jokes.

When it was time to go to bed, she said,
"Such a grand fellow as yourself, you can't sleep
on the floor."

So she made him up the spare bed.

And in the morning she woke him up with a cup
of coffee and a dram of whisky.

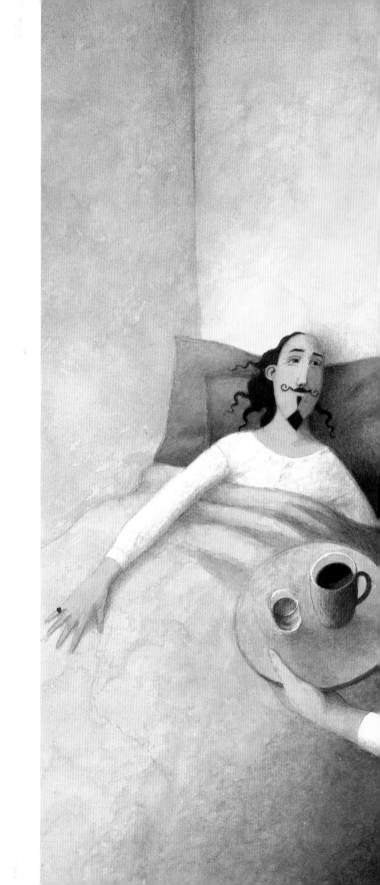

Finally, as he was standing on the doorstep about to leave she reached into her skirts, pulled out a gold coin and pressed it into his hand.

"Thank you," she said. "You've taught me something really useful. You've taught me how to make soup out of a nail."

"Well, it's really quite simple," he replied, "as long as you've got something good to add to it!"

Then he walked off down the path. He was just about to disappear from view when he turned back and gave her a wave.

She waved back, and said to herself: "You know, such people, they don't grow on every tree!"

And then she smiled. "Nail soup, indeed!"

Afterthought

Perhaps he didn't trick her after all.

But he softened her heart.

Maybe this was because they did two things

human beings have done since the beginning of time –

they shared food and told stories.

Long may we continue to do so!